The Gulls of the
EDMUND FITZGERALD

by Tres Seymour

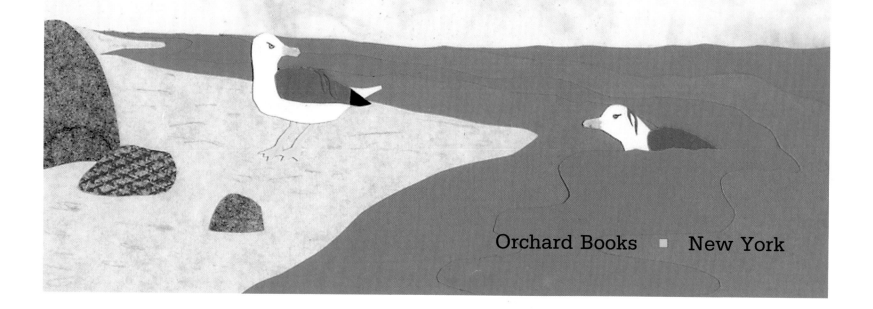

Orchard Books ■ New York

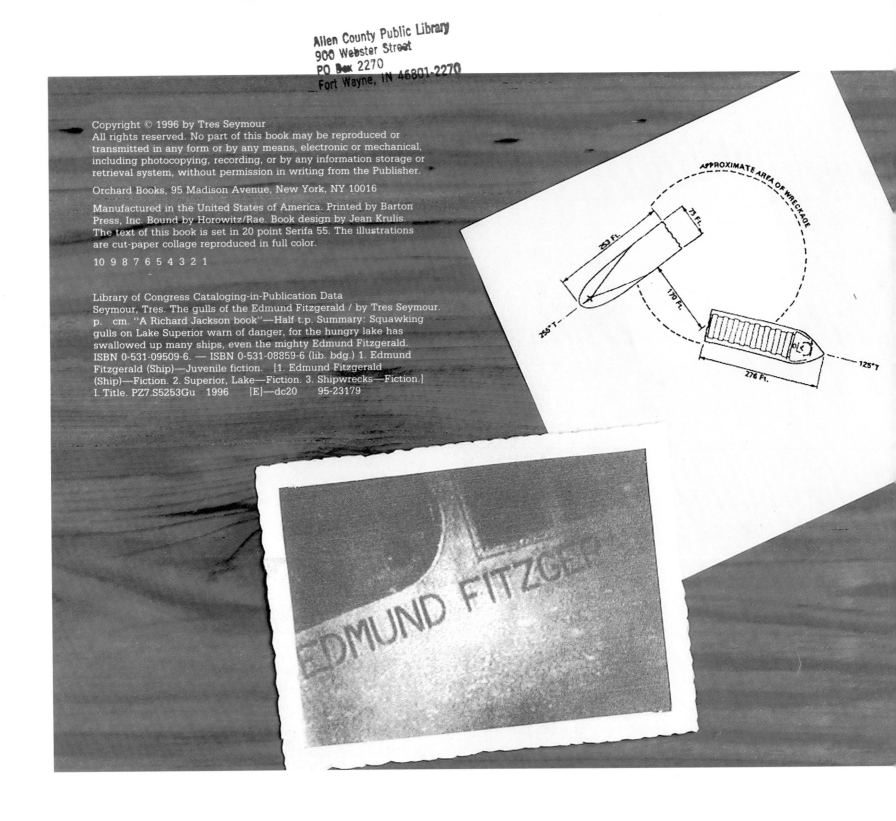

Orchard Books, 95 Madison Avenue, New York, NY 10016

Manufactured in the United States of America. Printed by Barton
Press, Inc. Bound by Horowitz/Rae. Book design by Jean Krulis.
The text of this book is set in 20 point Serifa 55. The illustrations
are cut-paper collage reproduced in full color.

10 9 8 7 6 5 4 3 2 1

Library of Congress Cataloging-in-Publication Data
Seymour, Tres. The gulls of the Edmund Fitzgerald / by Tres Seymour.
p.   cm. ''A Richard Jackson book''—Half t.p. Summary: Squawking
gulls on Lake Superior warn of danger, for the hungry lake has
swallowed up many ships, even the mighty Edmund Fitzgerald.
ISBN 0-531-09509-6. — ISBN 0-531-08859-6 (lib. bdg.) 1. Edmund
Fitzgerald (Ship)—Juvenile fiction. [1. Edmund Fitzgerald
(Ship)—Fiction. 2. Superior, Lake—Fiction. 3. Shipwrecks—Fiction.]
I. Title. PZ7.S5253Gu 1996   [E]—dc20   95-23179

In the absence of more definite information concerning the nature and extent of the difficulties and of problems other than those reported, and in the absence of any survivors or witnesses, the proximate cause of the loss of the S.S. Edmund Fitzgerald cannot be determined.

Department of Transportation, Coast Guard Marine Casualty Report USCG 16732P64216

MAP

of the

Great Lakes

and

Surrounding States

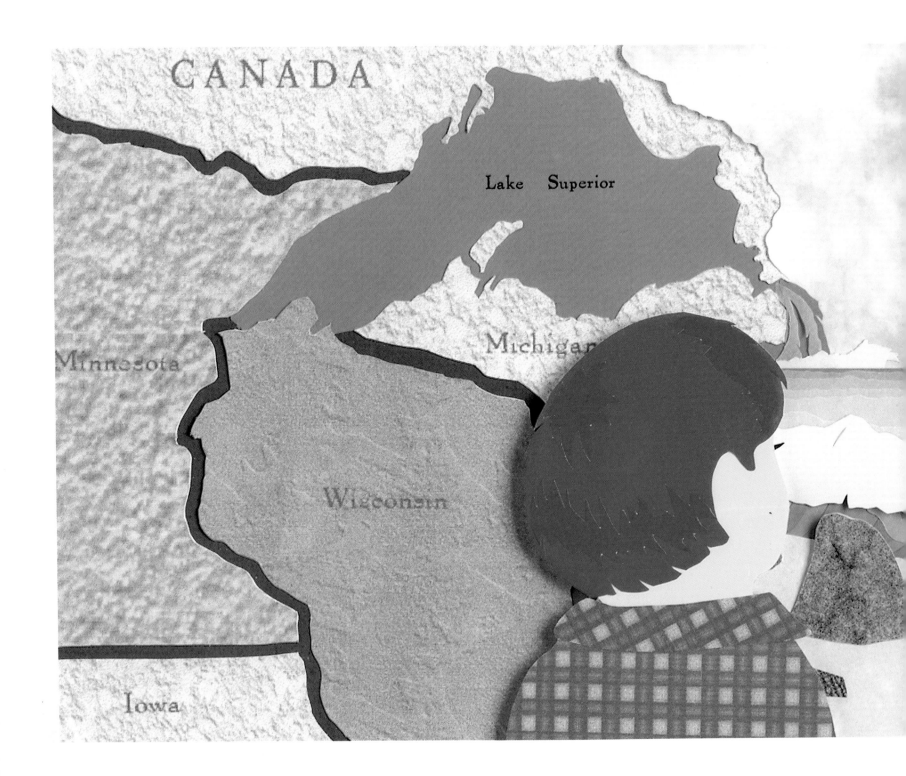

Once the Chippewa called this lake
Gitche Gumee,
but today we just say Superior.

I wanted to wade,
but the gulls on the rocks
cried out
when I took off
my shoe.

They said, "Don't go near! Don't go near!
Don't go near the water!"
"Why not?" I said, and the birds all stared,
first one eye, and then the other.

They said, "Superior has a hunger.

It swallowed the good ship *Sunbeam*.

Superior bared its winter teeth.
And the *Manistee*
went missing.

Superior reached
with frigid fingers.

They took the *City of Bangor*
to the bottom.

But the *Fitz!*
The *Fitzgerald!*
The *Edmund Fitzgerald!*

We are the gulls of the
Edmund Fitzgerald!

Seven hundred feet of hull
she sailed, Wisconsin to Ohio
in all weathers

Until the cruel, gray November

when the wind rose
and the waves reached up
and became the whole sky
and the sky fell like a wall

and the *Fitz*—

The *Fitzgerald!*

The *Edmund Fitzgerald!*

put her nose in the water
and drowned.
Hungry Superior split her
amidships—
the pride of the line!

Seven hundred feet of iron,
and a crew of twenty-nine.''

For a moment I saw faces
in the foamy waters—

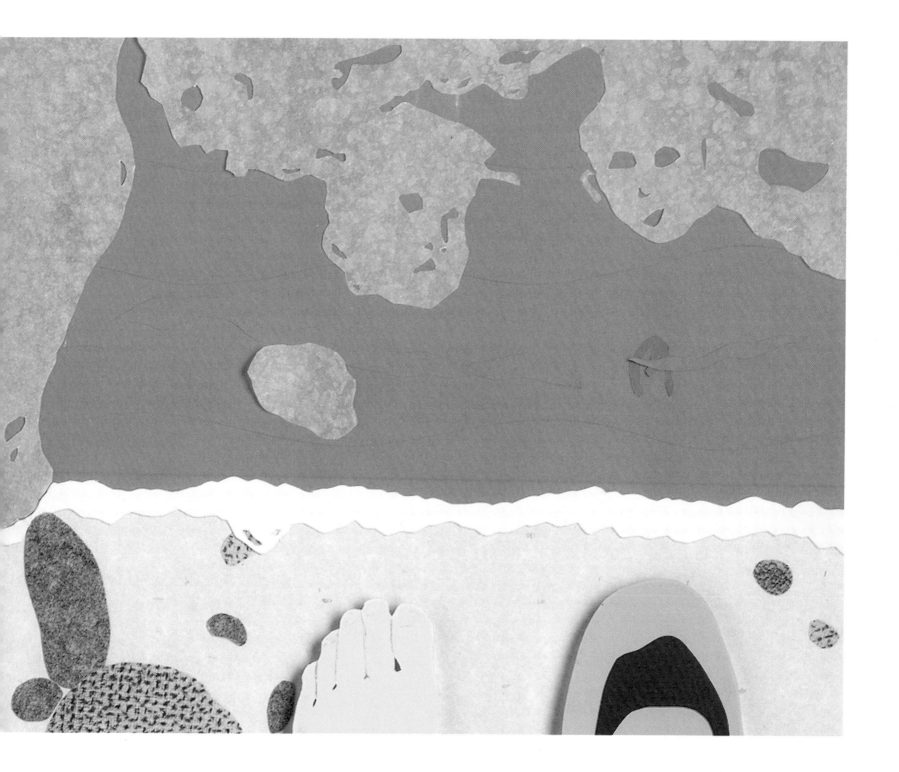

then a wave, like a tongue,

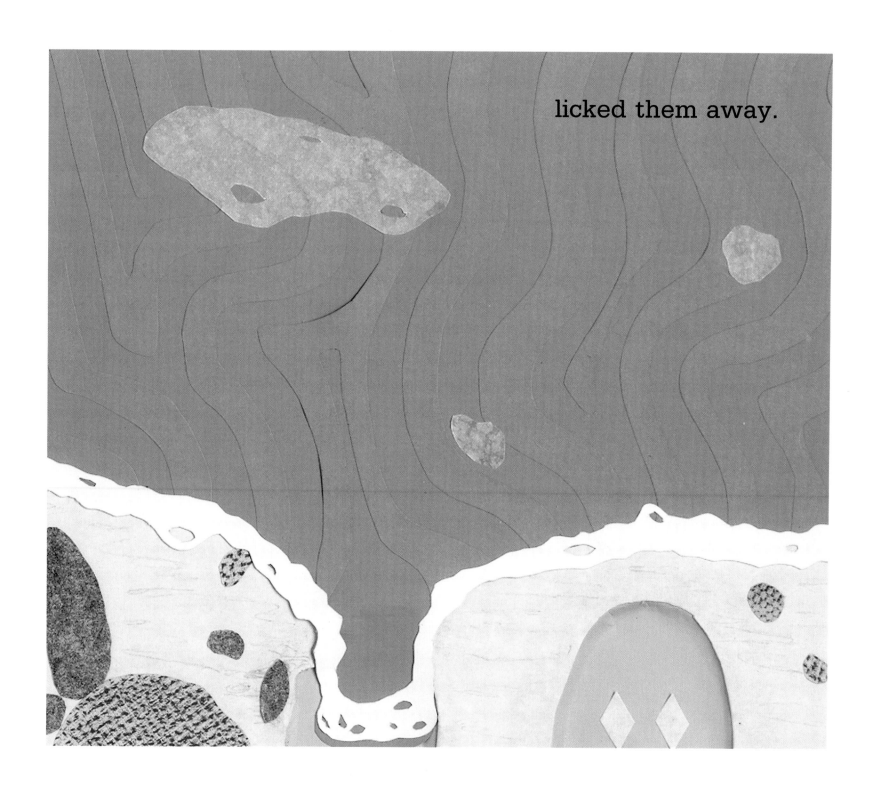

licked them away.

The gulls cried, "Don't go near! Don't go near!

Don't go near the water!

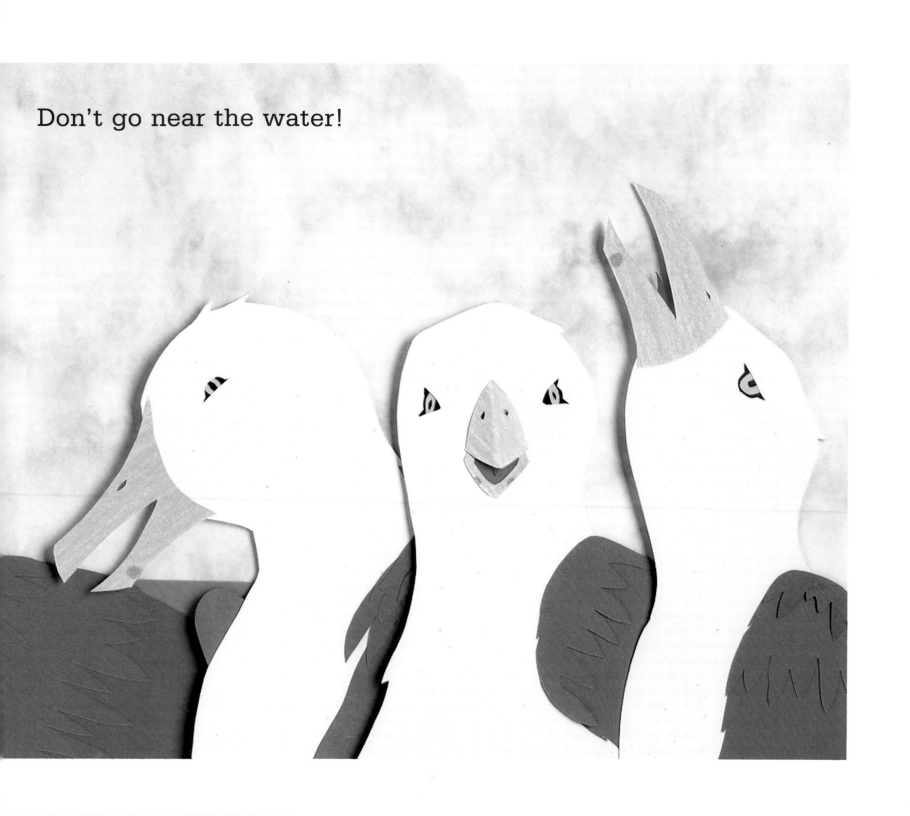

Superior has a muddy belly
where the *Fitz*—

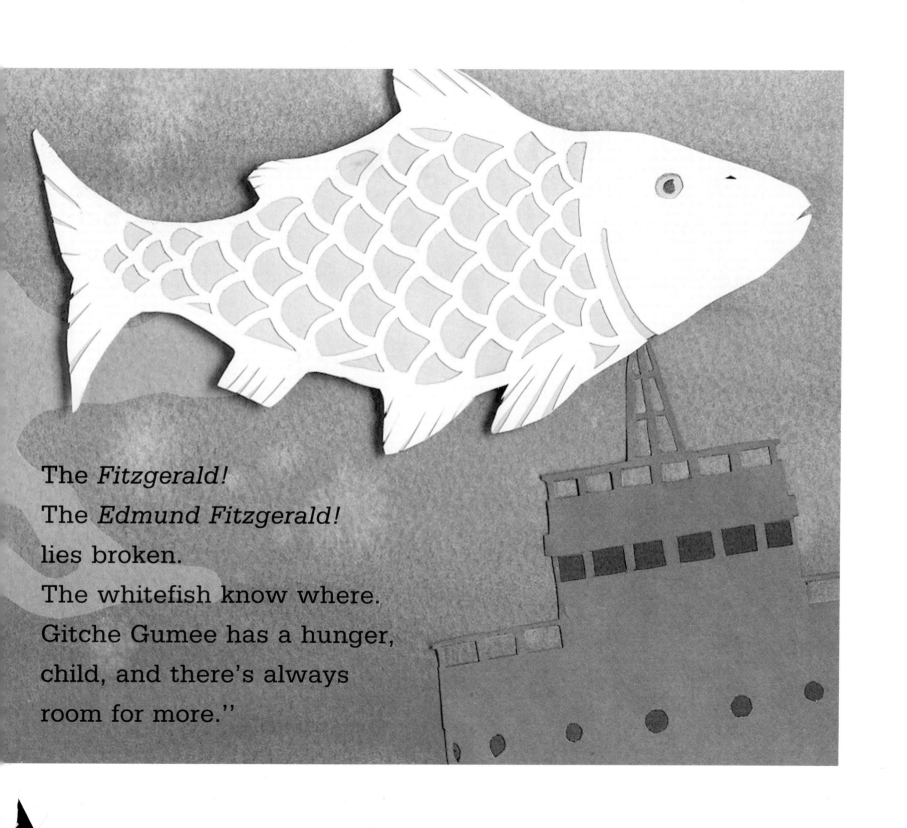

The *Fitzgerald!*
The *Edmund Fitzgerald!*
lies broken.
The whitefish know where.
Gitche Gumee has a hunger,
child, and there's always
room for more.''

Then the gulls, all cackling and flopping
their gray wings,
took off across the lake and dove

and did not come back.

But I could hear their calls
from below the waves—

The Fitz!
The Fitzgerald!
The Edmund Fitzgerald!
We are the gulls of the Edmund Fitzgerald!

Don't go near!